To my son, who is my one and only, my miracle baby.
To my parents, who have molded me into the person
I am today.
To my husband, who is my sidekick for life
(because every superhero needs one).
To my in-laws, who raised my husband to be
the man he is today.
To my friend Valerie, who encouraged me to turn this
idea into a reality.
To all moms, because we all have
Octo-Mommy's strength inside of us.

www.mascotbooks.com

Octo-Mommy

For more information, please contact:
Mascot Books
620 Herndon Parkway, Suite 320
Herndon, VA 20170
info@mascotbooks.com

Library of Congress Control Number: 2019920785

CPSIA Code: PRT0320A
ISBN-13: 978-1-64543-352-1

Printed in the United States

OCTO-MOMMY

Michele D. Pollak

Illustrated by Nidhom

Dana was an ordinary girl living in an ordinary world in a cozy, brick home with her loving husband, Grant, and her tiny, brave dog, Marshall.

Dana loved her job. Every day she played with children and helped them learn to talk. One day, as Dana pushed little Adam on the swing, he said, "Mama!" It was the first time he had spoken.

"Yay, Adam! You said 'Mama!'" It was a great start to a Monday morning. Dana thought this was going to be a good day.

Dana's next student, Melanie, was two and VERY opinionated. "Okay, sweetie. It's time to clean up the princesses," Dana said.

"NOOO! I want more play!" Melanie shouted and threw her water bottle right into Dana's nose. Smack! That really hurt.

Bradley was the sweetest two-year-old, but his nose was always running. As Dana turned to grab a box of tissues, Bradley picked his nose, reached out to her, and gently placed a bright green booger on her arm. Dana didn't even notice.

Later that afternoon, as Reid climbed out of
the ball pit, Dana noticed a bulge in his diaper.
She then got a HUGE whiff of it, and the room
started to smell like a farm. "Uh oh, Reid. Time
to take a potty break," she said to him as she
opened the window.

"Injury...boogers...poop," Dana sighed.

That night at dinner, Dana rambled about her day to her husband Grant. "I can STILL smell that poopy diaper! Then the kid who always has the runny nose sneezed all over me! I hope I don't get sick."

Grant chuckled, pointing at her arm. "You might want to go to the bathroom and wipe that off."

"Ewww! That little booger!" Dana giggled and ran off to the bathroom. Marshall pounced as food fell from Dana's lap. He was delighted!

The next morning, Dana wasn't feeling very well, so Grant took her to the doctor. It turned out Dana wasn't sick at all. As the doctor shared the good news, Dana and Grant shrieked,
"We're going to have a baby!"

As months passed, Dana's belly grew bigger while her worries grew stronger. Dana was so excited, but also very nervous. "What if my kid throws things at me? How do I change a stinky diaper? How can I tend to Marshall AND clean AND work AND take care of a baby? Am I going to be a good mom?" Suddenly, Dana felt a strange zap of energy run through her entire body. Slow twists and churns circled inside her stomach. Then she felt a hard punch on the left and a jab on the right. *Ouch! What was that? Could it be the baby?* "Nerves, it has to be nerves," she convinced herself.

In spite of her worries, Dana gently rubbed her belly and whispered, "I can't wait to meet you." Soon, baby Mason was born, and Dana finally became a mommy.

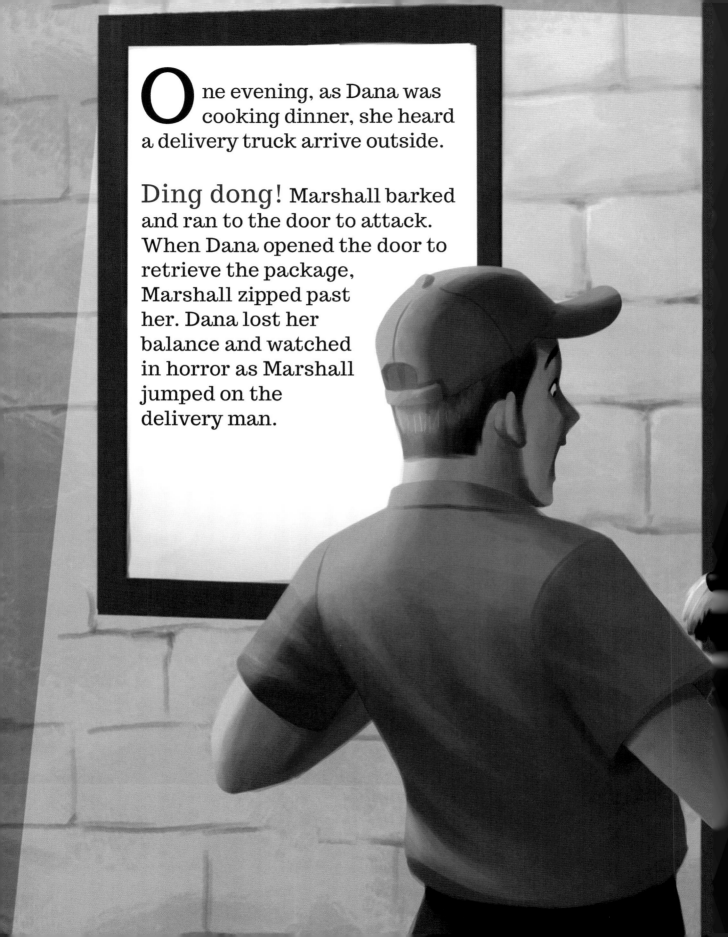

One evening, as Dana was cooking dinner, she heard a delivery truck arrive outside.

Ding dong! Marshall barked and ran to the door to attack. When Dana opened the door to retrieve the package, Marshall zipped past her. Dana lost her balance and watched in horror as Marshall jumped on the delivery man.

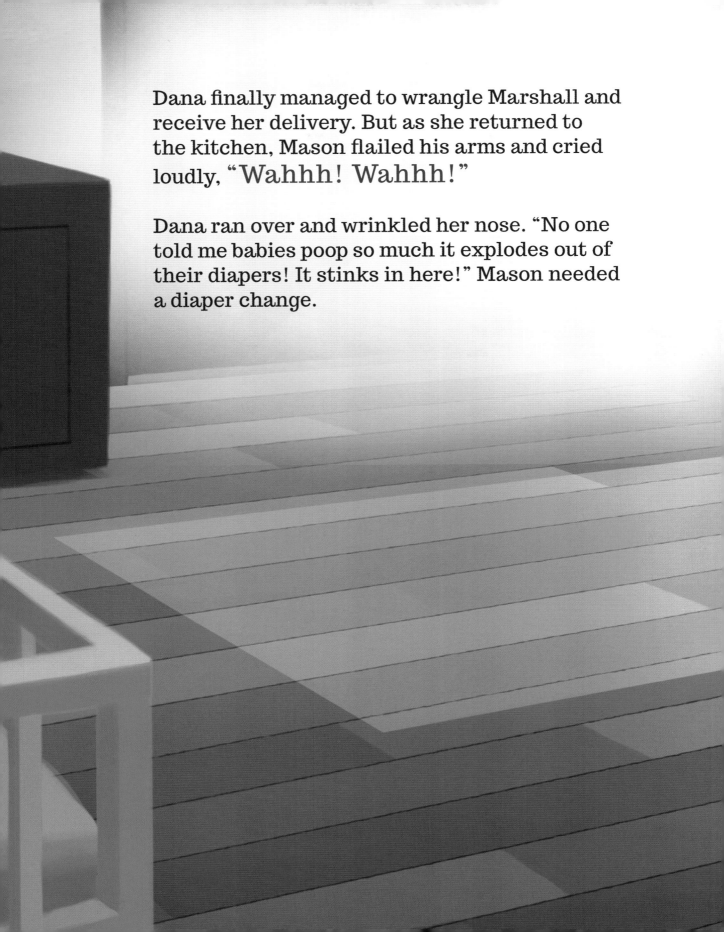

Dana finally managed to wrangle Marshall and receive her delivery. But as she returned to the kitchen, Mason flailed his arms and cried loudly, "Wahhh! Wahhh!"

Dana ran over and wrinkled her nose. "No one told me babies poop so much it explodes out of their diapers! It stinks in here!" Mason needed a diaper change.

But when Dana turned to fetch a new diaper, she noticed the water boiling over the pot. "Yikes!" Beep, beep! The dryer upstairs blared like a siren.

Bling, bling! Dana's boss sent an urgent email. Ring, ring! Dana's mom was calling again.

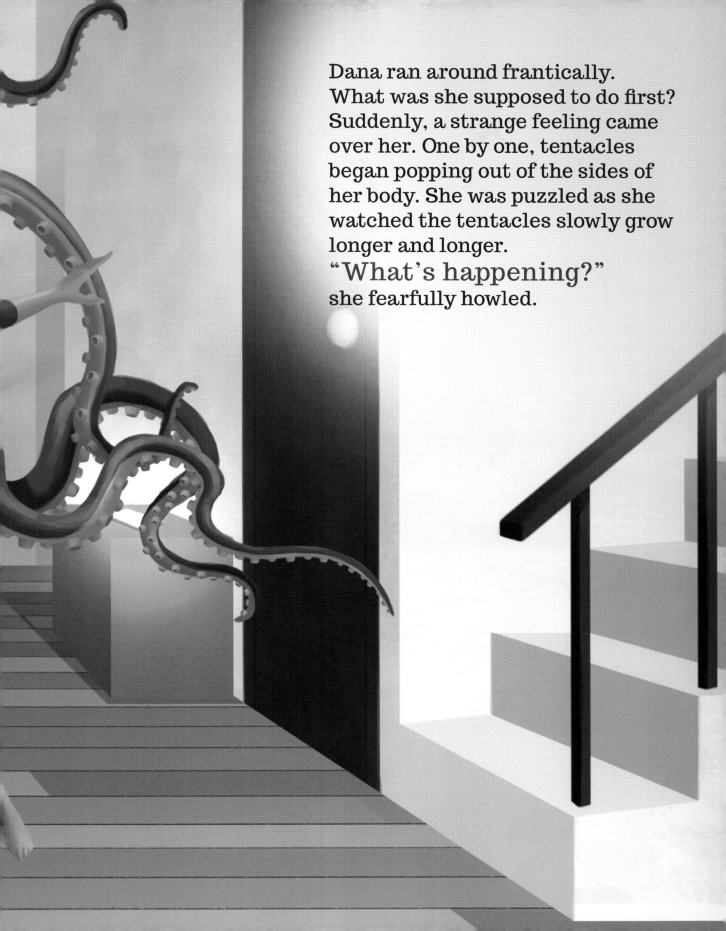

Dana ran around frantically.
What was she supposed to do first?
Suddenly, a strange feeling came
over her. One by one, tentacles
began popping out of the sides of
her body. She was puzzled as she
watched the tentacles slowly grow
longer and longer.
"What's happening?"
she fearfully howled.

One tentacle briskly slithered up the stairs and turned off the dryer. Another tentacle silenced her phone. A third one quickly turned the stove off and moved the boiling pot of water into the sink. A fourth tentacle rapidly typed an email to her boss.

An extra-long tentacle brought Marshall to Dana's side for emotional support. A pair of tentacles were on baby duty: one cleaned up Mason's stinky diaper while the other gave him a bottle. The final tentacle wiped Dana's worried forehead.

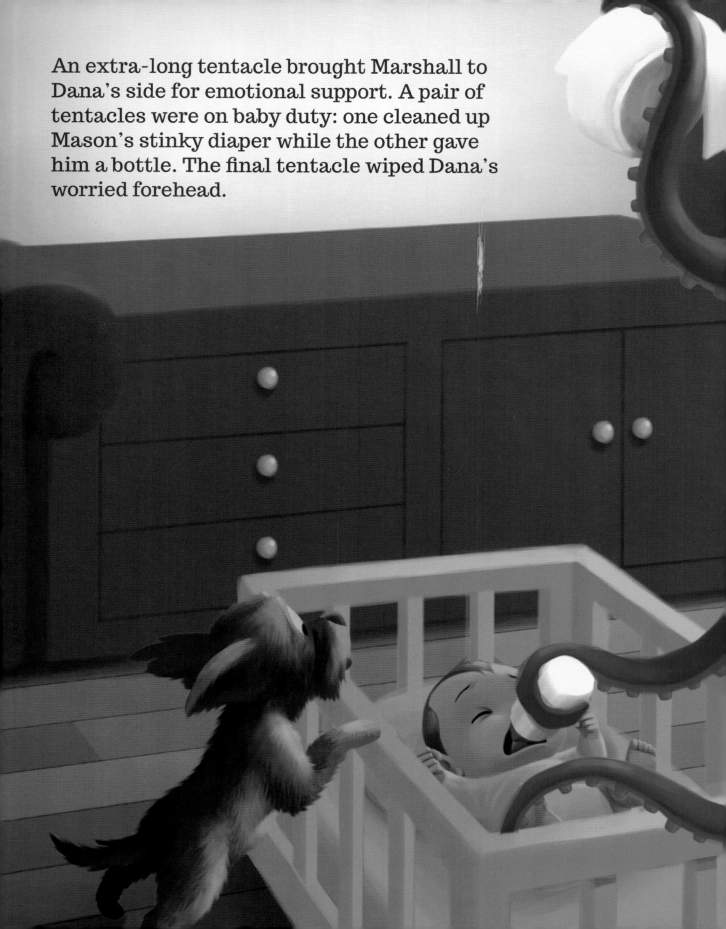

After all of the commotion settled, the tentacles slowly returned inside Dana's body. "What just happened?" she asked, turning to look at her reflection in the mirror.

Dana jumped as Grant came in the door. "Is everything okay?" he asked, looking around.

Dana hesitated but then confidently said, "It sure is. I have a pretty good handle on this mommy thing, ya' know."

Grant replied with a smile, "Of course. It's always been in you."

The next morning, Dana went grocery shopping with Mason. "Don't forget Marshall's dog bones," she reminded herself. But the box was all the way on the top shelf. Go figure!

As she reached up on her tip-toes, Mason's pacifier fell from his mouth. While Dana struggled to keep her balance, tentacles quickly popped out of her sides. One grabbed the box of dog bones, one steadied her body, and the other caught the pacifier mid-air.

"Wow, Mason! Mommy could get used to these extra hands! I mean tentacles," she giggled.

Dana came to realize that her capabilities were endless. She could handle commotion. She could handle chaos. She was now an extraordinary girl living in an ordinary world. And aren't all mommies extraordinary?

About the Author

Michele is a New Jersey native who resides in Washington, D.C. with her son, husband, and Yorkie. She received a B.A. in Speech and Hearing Sciences from The George Washington University and received a M.S. in Speech-Language Pathology from Loyola University Maryland. For more than a decade, Michele has practiced as a pediatric speech pathologist in school and private practice settings. She thoroughly enjoys educating parents, collaborating with teachers, and expanding children's communication skills. Her favorite aspect of work is engaging children and making them laugh. Although *Octo-Mommy* is a fictional story, Michele's creative inspiration stems from real life experiences as a mom. Motherhood is the job that she is most proud of and holds dearest to her heart.